I LOVE TO SHARE
أحبُ المشاركة

Shelley Admont
Illustrated by Sonal Goyal and Sumit Sakhuja

www.kidkiddos.com

Copyright©2014 by S. A. Publishing ©2017 by KidKiddos Books Ltd.

support@kidkiddos.com

First edition, 2017

Translated from English by Heba Salah Eldin

ترجمتهُ من الإنجليزية هبة صلاح الدين

Arabic editing by Shahad Sam and Sara Shoshaa

Library and Archives Canada Cataloguing in Publication Data

I Love to Share (Arabic Bilingual Edition)/ Shelley Admont

ISBN: 978-1-5259-0428-8 paperback

ISBN: 978-1-5259-0429-5 hardcover

ISBN: 978-1-5259-0427-1 eBook

Please note that the Arabic and English versions of the story have been written to be as close as possible. However, in some cases they differ in order to accommodate nuances and fluidity of each language.

Although the author and the publisher have made every effort to ensure the accuracy and completeness of information contained in this book, we assume no responsibility for errors, inaccuracies, omission, inconsistency, or consequences from such information.

KidKiddos Books

For those I love the most

إهداء لأولئك الذين أحبهم

"Look at how many new toys I have," said Jimmy the little bunny, looking around the room.

"انظر كم لعبة جديدة لدي" قال الأرنب الصغير جيمي وهو ينظر فى أرجاء الغرفة.

His birthday party was over and the room was full of presents.

قد انتهت حفلة عيد ميلاده و كانت الغرفة مليئة بالهدايا.

"Oh, your birthday party was so fun, Jimmy," his middle brother said.

قال أخوه الأوسط: " لقد كانت حفلة عيد ميلادك ممتعة جداً يا جيمي."

"Let's play," said his oldest brother. He took the largest box. "There's a huge train inside!"

قال أخوه الأكبر: "هيا نلعب" وقد أخذ أكبر صندوق هدايا وقال "إن بها قطاراً كبيراً!"

Suddenly, Jimmy jumped to his feet and grabbed the box. "Don't touch it! It's my train!" he cried. "All these presents are **MINE!**"

فجأة قفز جيمى واقفاً و جذب منه الصندوقِ بشدةٍ قائلاً: "لا تلمسه، إنه قطاري!" وصاح "كل هذه الهدايا ملكي!"

"But, Jimmy," said the oldest brother, "we always play together. What happened to you today?"

قال أخوه الأكبر "ولكن يا جيمي نحن دائماً نلعب سوياً، ماذا حدث لك اليوم؟"

"Today is MY birthday. And these are MY toys," Jimmy screamed.

صاح جيمي قائلاً: "اليوم عيد ميلادي أنا وهذه ألعابي أنا."

"We better go play basketball," said the oldest brother. He glanced out the window. "It's nice and sunny today."

قال أخوه الأكبر وهو ينظر من النافذة :"من الأفضل أن نلعب كرة السلة، فاليوم جميل ومشمس."

The two bunny brothers took a ball and went outside. Jimmy stayed in the room on his own.

أخذ أخوا جيمي الكرة و ذهبا للخارج، بينما ظل جيمي وحده فى الغرفة.

"Yeah!" he exclaimed. "Now all the toys are for me! I can do whatever I want!"

هتف جيمي قائلا: "مرحا! الآن كل اللعب لي! أستطيع أن أفعل كل ما أريد."

He took a large box and opened it happily. Inside he found a rail trail and a new colorful train. He just needed to put the rail trail together.

أخذ جيمى صندوقاً كبيراً وفتحه وهو سعيد. وجد بداخله قطاراً ملوناً جديداً و سكة القطار. كل ما كان عليه فعله هو أن يقوم بتركيب قطع سكة القطار.

"Oh, these pieces are too small!" he said, holding the rail trail parts. "How should I connect them together?"

قال جيمى وهو يمسك بقطع سكة القطار : "إن هذه القطع صغيرة جداً، كيف يمكننى أن أصِلها ببعضها البعض ؟"

Somehow he built the rail line, but it came out crooked. When he finally turned on his new colorful train, it got stuck on the track.

وبشكل ما، ركب جيمي سكة القطار، ولكنها كانت معوجة. وأخيراً و عندما شغل قطاره الجديد الملون، انحشر القطار على القضبان.

Jimmy looked around and spotted another box.

نظر جيمي حوله ولمح صندوقاً آخر.

"No worries. I have more new toys," he said and took another present. Inside there were superhero toys.

قال جيمي: "لا بأس، لازال لدى الكثير من اللعب الجديدة" و أخذ هديةً أخرى وكان بداخلها ألعابَ أبطالٍ خارقين.

"Wow!" exclaimed Jimmy. He started to run around the room with new superhero toys in his hands.

تعجب جيمي قائلاً: "رائع". بدأ جيمي فى اللعب والجري فى الغرفة ممسكاً بيديه بلعب الأبطال الخارقين.

Soon he became tired and bored. He tried everything. He played with his favorite teddy bear and he even opened all his presents, but it was not fun at all.

وسريعا ما أصبح مرهقاً و شعر بالملل. لقد جرب كل شيء، لقد لعب بدبه المفضل و فتح كل هداياه، ولكن لم يكن ذلك ممتعاً أبداً.

Jimmy watched through the window and saw his brothers playing cheerfully with their basketball. The sun was shining brightly, and they were laughing and enjoying themselves.

نظر جيمي من النافذة ورأى أخويه يلعبان كرة السلة بسعادة. كانت الشمس مشرقة وكانا يضحكان و يستمتعان بوقتهما.

"How are they having so much fun? They only have one basketball!" said Jimmy. "All the other toys are here with me."

قال جيمي: "كيف يمكنهما أن يستمتعا لهذا الحد! كل ما لديهما هو كرة واحدة فقط وباقي الألعاب معي هنا."

Then he heard a strange voice.

ومن ثم سمع صوتا غريبا.

"They SHARE," it said.

قال الصوت الغريب :" إنهما يتشاركان."

Jimmy looked around the room, staring at his bed where his teddy bear sat. The voice came from *there.* "What?" he whispered.

نظر جيمي في أرجاء الغرفة وحدّق باتجاه سريره حيث جلس الدب اللعبة. لقد أتى الصوت الغريب من هناك. فهمس له جيمي "ماذا ؟"

"They share," repeated his teddy bear with a smile.

"إنهما يتشاركان" أعادها الدب اللعبة قائلاً بإبتسامة.

Jimmy looked at him amazed. He never thought that sharing could be fun.

نظر إليه جيمي مندهشا. فلم يعتقد أبداً أن المشاركة شيء ممتع.

He shook his head. "No...I don't like to share. I love my toys."

هزّ جيمي رأسه نافيا وقال: "لا... أنا لا أحب أن أشارك الأخرين. أنا أحب ألعابي."

"Try it," insisted his teddy bear. "Just try it."

"حاول" أصر الدب اللعبة. "فقط جرب."

Meanwhile the weather changed. Dark clouds covered the sky and large raindrops started falling to the ground.

وفى هذه الأثناء، بدأ الجو يتغير. غطت السماءَ سحبٌ كثيفة وبدأت قطرات مطر كبيرة فى السقوط على الأرض.

Laughing, the two bunny brothers ran into the house.

ركض الأرنبان الأخوان إلى المنزل وهما يضحكان.

"Oh, you're all wet," said Mom. "Go change your clothes and I'll make you hot chocolate."

قالت الأم : "يا إلهي إنكما مبتلان تماماً. غيرا ملابسكما وسأعد لكما مشروب الشوكولاتة الساخن."

"Come, Jimmy, do you want hot chocolate too?" she asked. Jimmy nodded.

سألت الأم جيمي : "هيا يا جيمى، هل تريد مشروب الشوكولاتة الساخن أيضاً ؟" فأومأ جيمي برأسه.

Mom opened the fridge to grab the milk. "Look, there's a small piece of your birthday cake left."

وعندما فتحت الأم الثلاجة لتأخذ الحليب قالت "انظر، لازال هناك قطعة صغيرة متبقية من كعكة عيد ميلادك."

Jimmy jumped to his feet. "Yeah, can I have it? It was so tasty!"

قفز جيمى قائلاً "مرحا!، هل يمكنني أن آخذها؟ لقد كانت لذيذة جداً؟"

At that moment, his brothers entered the kitchen.

وفى هذا الوقت دخل أخواه إلى المطبخ.

"Did you say cake?" asked the middle brother.

قال أخوه الأوسط :"هل قلت كعكة؟"

"I'd like a piece," added the oldest brother.

و قال أخوه الأكبر: "أريد قطعة."

Their father followed them. "Is this a...birthday cake?"

تبعهم والدهم "هل هذه كعكة عيد الميلاد حقا؟"

Mom smiled softly. "Ahh...there is actually a tiny little piece left. And there are five of us."

ابتسمت الأم إبتسامة خفيفة وقالت: "آه.. في الحقيقة لقد تبقت قطعة صغيرة جداً، ونحن خمسة!"

Jimmy looked at his loving family and felt a warm feeling spread from his heart. He knew what he needed to do and it felt so good.

نظر جيمي إلى عائلته المُحبة وشعر بدفءٍ فى قلبِه. لقد عرف الآن

ما يجب عليه فعله وقد شعر بشعورٍ جميلٍ.

"We can share," he said. "Let's cut it into five pieces."

قال جيمي: "يمكننا أن نتشارك. لنقطعها إلى خمسة أجزاء."

All the members of the bunny family nodded their heads. Then they sat around the table and everyone enjoyed a piece of birthday cake and a hot chocolate.

وافق جميع أفراد العائلة، ثم جلسوا جميعا حول المائدة واستمتع كل

واحد منهم بقطعة من الكعكة و مشروب الشوكولاتة الساخن.

Jimmy glanced at their smiling faces and thought, *Sharing can actually feel very nice after all.*

نظر جيمي إلى وجوههم المبتسمة و أدرك أن المشاركة يمكن حقاً ان تكون شيئاً جميلاً.

When they finished, Mom came to Jimmy and gave him a huge hug. "Happy birthday, honey," she said.

و عندما انتهوا قامت والدة جيمي و عانقته عناقا كبيرا و قالت له: "عيد ميلاد سعيد يا عزيزي."

The two older brothers and their dad gathered around them and shared the family hug.

و التف أخواه والأب حولهما وشاركاهما العناق.

"Happy birthday, Jimmy," they screamed together.

و صاح الجميع: "كل عام و أنت بخير يا جيمي."

Jimmy smiled. "Do you want to play with my toys?" he asked his brothers. "I have a new train and new superheroes."

ابتسم جيمي وسأل أخويه: "هل تريدان أن تلعبا بألعابي الجديدة؟

لدي قطارٌ جديد و أبطال خارقون أيضاً."

"Yeah! Let's play!" shouted the bunny brothers.

قال الأخوة الأرانب فرحين: "نعم.. هيا نلعب!"

Together Jimmy and his brothers built a perfect rail trail. The train whistled and ran fast around the track.

ركّب جيمى مع أخويه سكة القطار بشكل مثالي. صفر القطار و جرى سريعاً على القضبان.

Then they opened the presents and played with all their toys.

ثم فتحوا الهدايا ولعبوا بكل الألعاب.

From then on, Jimmy loved to share. He even said that sharing is fun!

و منذ ذلك الحين، أحبّ جيمي المشاركة. حتى أنه قال أن المشاركة ممتعة.

CPSIA information can be obtained
at www.ICGtesting.com
Printed in the USA
LVHW071623231219
641482LV00021B/537/P